A Bigger Digger

Brett Avison · Craig Smith

The Five Mile Press

The Five Mile Press
1 Centre Road, Scoresby, Victoria 3179, Australia
www.fivemile.com.au

Text copyright © Brett Avison, 2011
Illustrations copyright © Craig Smith, 2011
ISBN 9781743002056 (pbk)
All rights reserved
First published 2011
Printed in China 5 4 3 2

They were doing no **harm**
on **Mum's** little farm,
just **digging** around in
the shade.

With **Oscar's** front paws
and **Bryn** on all fours,
working hard with his
bucket and **spade.**

Right there in the yard
they struck **something** hard,

as they dug down it kept getting **bigger.**

There's a **dinosaur** head
in the **shade** by the shed.
I need a much **bigger digger!**

'The **museum** said
they're sending round **Ted,**
with a **bobcat** and **truck** for the tailings.'

'I've come to take **charge**,
this hole could get **large**.
The shed's **got to go**,
and the railings.'

'What I **thought** was a boulder
was really a **shoulder!**
We have to go **deeper**, I figure.'

'We'll need **trucks** and more men.
And I've called my mate **Ken**,
he's got a much **bigger digger!**

Ted was **looking** quite pale.
'There's a **spine** and a **tail!**'
Bryn's mum sat him **down** with a drink.

'Well, **Oscar**. Well, Bryn,'
Ted said with a **grin**.
'Come sit here with me while I **think**.'

'It might be **complete**!
Let's **go** for the feet!
There's certainly not been **another**.'

'You'll be **famous**, you'll see!
You'll be on **TV**.
Oscar, and **you**, and your **mother**!'

'We'll need **much** more space,
for **mounting** in place.
We'll go **wider** and **deeper** and
bigger.'

'We'll need some **backhoes**
and **trucks** by the rows.
And you guessed it —
a much **bigger digger!**'

But why was Bryn's shirt
all **covered** in dirt?
Why was Oscar **hiding** a snigger?

'Do dinosaurs have **daddies,** Ted?
We've just **found** a larger head.'

Also available

Stuck In the Muck

On Mum and Ted's farm there's a very large barn, where Milky the cow was a pet. But no-one could guess how she got herself stuck in the mud on a rain-sodden night.
Join Bryn, Oscar and a parade of machines — and broken gear — as they help Milky out of the muck.

A funny, light-hearted story with a surprise twist at the end.